SCREAM STREET

Book One

FANG OF THE VAMPIRE

SCREAM STREET

Book One
FANG OF THE VAMPIRE

TOMMY DONBAVAND

CANDLEWICK PRESS

visit us at www.abdopublishing.com

Reinforced library bound edition published in 2012 by Spotlight, a division of the ABDO Group, PO Box 398166, Minneapolis, Minnesota 55439. Spotlight produces high-quality reinforced library bound editions for schools and libraries. Published by agreement with Candlewick Press. www.candlewick.com

Printed in the United States of America, North Mankato, Minnesota.
102011
012012
This book contains at least 10% recycled materials.

Library of Congress Cataloging-in-Publication Data

This title was previously cataloged with the following information:

Donbavand, Tommy.
Fang of the vampire / by Tommy Donbavand.
p.   cm. — (Scream Street ; 1)
Summary: When Luke Watson turns into a werewolf for the third time, he and his parents are moved to Scream Street, where they and other "unusual lifeforms" are trapped unless Luke and his friends can find six powerful relics hidden by the founding fathers before sinister landlord, Sir Otto, does.
[1. Horror stories. 2. Werewolves—Fiction. 3. Vampires—Fiction.
4. Zombies—Fiction. 5. Books and reading—Fiction.]   I. Title. II. Series.
PZ7.D7162Fan 2010
[Fic]—dc22

3 1969 01168 5350

ISBN 978-1-59961-992-7 (reinforced library edition)

All Spotlight books are reinforced library bindings
and manufactured in the United States of America.

For Mum: Here are the keys to
the biggest house on Scream Street.

Meet the residents

Luke Watson

Cleo Farr

Resus Negative

Dixon

Sir Otto Sneer

Samuel Skipstone

Alston and Bella Negative

Eefa Everwell

Doug

Dr. Skully

Niles Farr

Mr. and Mrs. Watson

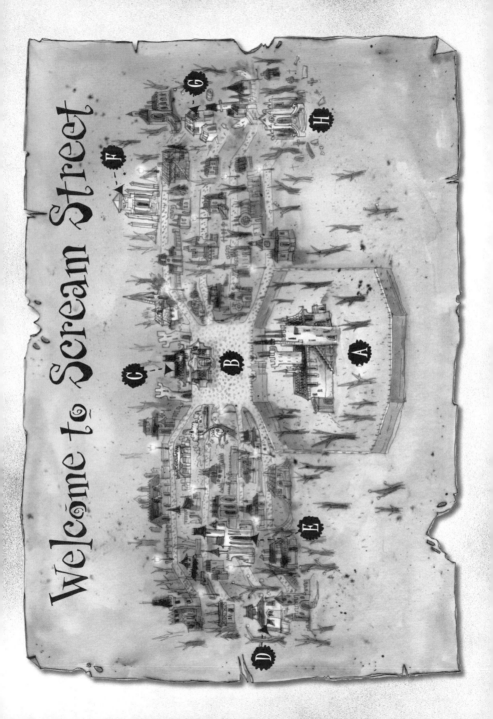

Who lives where

A Sheer Hall

B Central Square

C Everwell's Emporium

D No. 13: Luke Watson

E No. 14: Resus Negative

F No. 22: Cleo Farr

G No. 28: Doug, Turf, and Berry

H No. 39: The Skullys

Chapter One
The Chase

The schoolboy leaped over the wall into the graveyard, his feet skidding on wet grass. Barely managing to keep his balance, he ran on, dodging between headstones that jutted from the ground like rotten teeth.

Behind him, the creature landed in the mud, still transforming. It roared as its razor-sharp claws ripped through the black leather of its shoes and glinted in the weak sunlight. Tearing away what remained of its footwear with yellowing nails, the monster gave chase.

The boy tripped and fell, banging his head on a gravestone. A flash of white filled his vision, and he was temporarily stunned. Forcing himself to stand, the schoolboy rubbed at the cut on his forehead. As he was staring at the red liquid smeared across his fingertips, he heard a snarl.

The creature was in front of him now, approaching, its eyes never leaving his own. The boy was reminded of nature shows on TV in which lions stalked their prey. He stepped back and found himself pressed against the cold marble of an ornate headstone. He was trapped.

The creature screamed as its face began to push outward, bones splintering noisily and quickly reforming, muscles tearing, then instantly knotting together as its entire head changed shape. Strands of thick fur pushed out of every pore of its skin.

Then the fully formed werewolf lifted its snout to the sky and howled.

 2

"N-no!" stuttered the schoolboy. "Please don't hurt me!" He tried to run, but the werewolf was on him in a second, lashing out with its claws.

Four crimson lines soaked into the material of the boy's torn white school shirt as he fell to the ground once again. He pushed himself backward across the muddy grass as the monster sniffed at the air, the scent of blood filling its nostrils. Baring its teeth, the wolf prepared to leap on its victim.

Suddenly a yapping sound distracted the creature, and it spun to see a small chihuahua bounding around its legs and nipping at its back paws. In the distance a voice could be heard calling out, "Fluffy! Here, boy!"

The monster kicked the yelping dog away and turned back to its prey. As the schoolboy screamed, the chihuahua bit the werewolf hard on the leg, then disappeared into the bushes.

Roaring with rage, the wolf turned and raced after the dog.

Chapter Two
The Move

Luke Watson turned the dog collar over in his hands, wiping dried blood from the name tag to reveal the word FLUFFY. The chihuahua had wriggled out of its collar and run away as the werewolf caught hold of it, a cut on the ear the only evidence that it had been in a fight at all.

Hearing a sound on the stairs, Luke stuffed the collar under his pillow and grabbed the game-pad of his computer console, resuming his battle against the evil mechanoids. "Come in," he called in response to a quiet tap on his bedroom door.

His mom entered, carrying a tray of food. Luke glanced at the meal: vegetarian again. His parents hadn't cooked him meat for almost a year now.

"Got onto the next level yet?" his mom asked, putting the tray down on the desk.

Luke shook his head. "I've gotten rid of the robot generals, but I need to kill the overlord before I can progress to the mother ship."

Mrs. Watson sat down on the bed. She said nothing for a while, then softly cleared her throat. "I spoke to Steven Black's parents."

"I thought Dad was going to call them."

"He's not back from work yet," explained his mom.

Luke tried unsuccessfully to hide the irritation in his voice. "Figures!"

"Steven told his parents he hurt his chest

 6

climbing over a barbed wire fence," said his mom.

Luke concentrated on the game, silent.

"Why him, Luke? You've got few enough friends at school as it is."

"He's no friend!" snapped Luke, throwing the gamepad onto the bed. "He's a bully! He stole some girl's bag on the way home from school; I was just trying to get it back for her. There was no reason for him to turn on me!"

"He didn't know what would happen," said his mom. "He didn't know that you would . . ." She sighed, leaving the sentence unfinished. "The scratches aren't deep," she said. "It's going to be OK. This time."

Luke studied his mom as she picked up the gamepad and did her best to fight a battalion of robots wielding laser guns. Neither of his parents had smiled for a long time. Not since he had first transformed into a werewolf.

"You know," he said with a grin, "you suck at this game!" Mrs. Watson punched him play-fully on the arm as he snatched the controls from her. "You only ever press one button at a time. But if you press a combination—"

A smash came from downstairs.

*   *   *

Luke bounded down the stairs two at a time and skidded to halt. The living room and hall were full of blond-haired men packing the family's belongings into crates and carrying furniture out of the house. Each wore a shimmering purple jumpsuit with G.H.O.U.L. printed across the back.

One of the men was clearing up the remains of a broken vase. Luke's dad, just home from work, was struggling to pull the pieces away from him. The man simply raised a hand and pressed it over Mr. Watson's eyes. Luke watched in terror as his dad crumpled to the floor.

"Mike!" yelled Luke's mom, rushing in. She dropped to her knees beside her husband and grabbed his wrist, checking for a pulse. The blond man laid his palm over her face, and she, too, collapsed, with a moan.

Luke raced across the room, fighting to get to his parents. One of the men gripped his arm and pulled him back so that two of his colleagues could pass by with a large picture. They stepped over Mr. and Mrs. Watson as if they were nothing more than lumps in the carpet.

Luke grabbed the shoulder of the man whose

8

touch had knocked out his parents, spinning him around. "What have you—?" The words stuck in his throat.

The man's head had no features—no eyes, nose, ears, or mouth. Just a smooth layer of skin. Luke glanced around the room. All the men were the same.

"Who are you?" he demanded, backing away. He fell onto the sofa, kicking out as the man pressed three fingertips to the side of his head. Luke suddenly became aware of a voice flooding his mind.

"We are the Movers," said the voice. "You are being moved."

Luke stared up into the featureless face. "Why?"

"You attacked a boy."

"But he got away when I"—Luke stumbled over his words—"when the wolf chased the chihuahua! He won't tell anyone about me, honest!"

The explanation made no difference. The Mover pulled his hand away and turned to pick up a framed photograph. Luke jumped to his feet and dashed after the man, stopping as he noticed that his parents had gone.

"Where are they?" he shouted. "What have you done with my parents?"

The sound of a zipper being closed caught his attention, and Luke dashed to the kitchen to discover another Mover sealing his mom inside a purple bag. An identical bag, presumably containing his dad, lay on the table.

"Let them go!" he screamed, launching himself

at the faceless man and trying to unzip the bag. Luke didn't see the second Mover until his hand covered Luke's face and the world dissolved into a fizzing pool of purple light.

Luke woke up in near darkness. He was lying on his bed, a dull pain throbbing behind his eyes. Groaning, he reached for the glass of water on his bedside table. A few gulps cleared his dry throat, and he sat upright.

Luke froze. He was on his bed, but this wasn't his room. A large glass chandelier hung from the high ceiling above him. The walls were painted green, and the floor was a dark polished wood. A purple bag, smaller than the ones in which he had seen his parents wrapped, lay over the end of the bed.

The tray with his dinner on it sat beside his homework on the desk, and the game console was in its place on top of the now dark computer monitor. Luke leaned over and pressed the ON switch, but the screen didn't seem to be working. He slid his hand beneath his pillow and pulled out the blood-soaked dog collar. All his stuff was here; this just wasn't his bedroom.

Luke swung his legs off the bed, stuffing the

dog collar into his pocket. He found his sneakers and slipped them on, then went over to the bookshelf and ran his fingers over his books to check that they were all real. They were.

Luke opened the heavy door and found himself standing at the top of an ornately carved stairway. A thick black rug at his feet appeared to be moving, and it was a moment before Luke realized that he was looking at hundreds of spiders. They crawled across the landing as one, dragging tiny webbing sacks of dust and leaving behind a trail of clean red carpet. The spiders were vacuuming.

Luke crossed the landing and checked inside the other rooms on the top floor of the house. His parents' bedroom was as it should be, their wrought-iron bedstead and their bureaus all in place. Two purple body bags lay, discarded, on the bedroom floor.

The bathroom was basic, with a bare stone floor and an ancient bathtub. Gas lamps hung from the walls. Luke was reaching out to test one when he heard muffled voices.

He headed downstairs and found a living room lined with dark wood paneling; the family's brightly colored sofa looked out of place in such

 12

ornate surroundings. Spiders were at work here, too, cleaning the deep-pile carpet.

Hearing the voices again, Luke went back out into the hallway. He pushed open a door on his right to reveal an old kitchen. His parents were sitting together at one end of a long wooden table.

"Mom!" yelled Luke as he ran across the kitchen and flung his arms around her. She was shaking. "Where are we?"

"We don't know," said Luke's dad. "We woke up and found ourselves on our bed in some room upstairs. We found you but couldn't wake you up."

"And we're wearing these," added Mrs. Watson, holding up her arm to reveal a bracelet like those used for hospital patients, stamped with the number 13. Luke checked his own wrist and discovered an identical band.

Someone hammered at the front door.

"Stay here," said Luke. He tore the strip of paper from his wrist and dashed back out into the hallway.

"Luke, no!" His mom grabbed for his arm, but he was already leaving the room.

Three figures were silhouetted against the frosted glass of the front door. Luke approached cautiously, then slid back the solid brass bolts and opened the door just enough to peer out into the cold air.

"Welcome to Scream Street!" boomed a voice. Luke swallowed hard. Standing on the doorstep was a family of vampires.

Chapter Three
The Attack

The tallest vampire
threw aside his cape,
grabbed Luke's hand,
and shook it furiously.
"Alston Negative's the
name. This is my wife,
Bella, and our son,
Resus!"

"We're your new neighbors," said the woman, striding past Luke toward the kitchen doorway. Mr. and Mrs. Watson stood there, mouths open.

"No!" Luke shouted, struggling to free himself from the handshake. Before he could move, the female vampire had reached beneath her cape and produced a vase of dead roses, handing the gift to Luke's mom. Thick red liquid filled the container. It was blood.

Mrs. Watson paled. Luke ran, catching her just as she began to faint. The vase smashed to the floor, spraying blood up the walls. The younger vampire darted past his father and helped Luke to sit his mom on the stairs, wafting his cape in front of her face.

Luke studied the boy. He looked about the same age as himself, although he had jet-black hair and white skin with dark rings around his eyes. Sharp fangs protruded from the boy's mouth.

"Are you a real vampire?" Luke asked.

Resus stared at him. "What do you think?"

"Why don't you two boys head upstairs and play?" said Bella, stepping in to take charge of

 16

Mrs. Watson. "We'll clean up and make sure your mom is all right."

"I think I should stay," said Luke, squeezing his mom's hand as she came around from her faint.

"It's OK," said Mr. Watson. "I think we need to find out what's going on."

"If you're sure . . ." said Luke, checking for the slightest indication that his parents wanted him to remain with them. Mr. Watson nodded, and Luke reluctantly led Resus Negative up to his room.

Resus grabbed a gory horror novel from the bookshelf and flopped onto the bed to read. Luke closed the door and watched the young vampire for a moment. "So, are you going to bite my neck and suck my blood?"

Resus didn't look up. "Not unless you annoy me."

Luke took a deep breath. What type of conversation did you have with a vampire? "Have you read that one before?" he asked, gesturing toward the book.

"We're not backward here, you know," said Resus, turning the page.

"I didn't mean that. I just thought . . ."

There was an awkward silence. Luke noticed black droplets trickling down the vampire's neck. "Your hair dye is running."

Resus spun around, pulling his cape up higher around his neck. "It's not dye!" he snapped. "My hair is naturally this color! All vampires have black hair."

"I was just saying," replied Luke. "Check it in the mirror if you like."

"I can't," growled Resus. "I'm a vampire. I don't have a reflection."

"But I can see your reflection," said Luke, pointing to the mirror above his desk.

Resus slammed the book closed. "Look, I'm not happy about being sent up here either," he said, "but my dad asked me to be nice to you." He opened the book again as if to continue reading. "I thought you were going to be another vampire or, at the very least, a troll. But you're just a normal. G.H.O.U.L. had no business bringing you here."

"G.H.O.U.L.!" gasped Luke. "That was written on the backs of the faceless men. What does it mean?"

"Government Housing of Unusual Life-forms," muttered Resus. "And by 'faceless men,' I presume you mean the Movers?"

"You've seen them?" asked Luke.

"They're everywhere when we have a new family move in," said Resus. "Although I think they went to the wrong address this time."

Luke sighed. Unusual life-forms. Is that what people thought of him now? "What's a normal?" he asked.

Resus turned another page. "You don't know anything, do you? *You're* a normal! Someone from the outside. Someone who doesn't belong here."

Luke turned to gaze out the window. Resus pulled a can of black hairspray from inside his cloak and gave his bangs a quick blast.

"I'm a werewolf," said Luke.

Resus stuffed the can back inside his cape. "For real?"

"I first transformed a year ago, on my birthday," explained Luke. "My parents thought I was having some sort of fit until the claws appeared."

"Do I have to beware of you when there's a full moon?" asked the vampire.

Luke shook his head. "That's just in movies. I change whenever I get angry."

"And that's what happened the first time?"

"My dad missed my party because he was working late," said Luke. "When he came home, I remember shouting at him, then nothing else. Next thing I know, I'm strapped to a hospital bed being injected with everything the doctors can find." Luke stared at the ghostly reflection of himself in the window. "That's when they told me I'd attacked my dad."

"Did you hurt him?" asked Resus.

"It would have been worse, but my parents managed to tie me up. If they hadn't, I don't know what I—"

A book bounced off the back of Luke's head and he spun around angrily. "What was that for?" he shouted.

"That wasn't me!" said Resus. "It just flew across the room!"

"Yeah, right," said Luke. "A book jumped off the desk by itself and hit me."

"It's true!" said Resus. As he spoke, Luke's desk lamp rose into the air. The vampire ducked as the lamp smashed against the wall behind him.

Within seconds, everything was moving: books, CDs, games—each item taking flight. Luke raced for the door. "What's happening?"

"It's a poltergeist attack!" said Resus as the tray of cold food hit him full in the face. "Lentil bake?" he asked scornfully.

Luke dodged a thick science textbook. "I'd kill for a cheeseburger!"

The boys dashed downstairs to discover the two older vampires in the kitchen, doing their best to protect Luke's parents from soaring items of furniture.

"Dad! What can we do?" yelled Resus, jumping as a chair whizzed past.

"Go to Everwell's!" shouted Alston. "See if Eefa has finished that spell yet."

Nodding, Resus ran for the open front door, then disappeared into the darkness beyond. With a glance back at his mom and dad, Luke followed.

Outside, Luke got his first look at Scream Street. Number 13, his new home, was tall and mis-shapen, towering high into the air. Its black slate roof appeared to almost pierce the thick gray clouds lurking above.

Gas lamps flickered on the tops of iron posts, casting spindly shadows of the dead trees that punctuated the sidewalk. A cold wind howled, banging gates and slamming window shutters.

"What's Everwell's?" asked Luke, catching up with Resus.

"Everwell's Emporium," explained the vampire. "Eefa Everwell is a witch. She's been working on a spell to stop the poltergeist attacks."

"Polter*what* attacks?" asked Luke, pulling Resus into a bush as a metal trash can shot along the sidewalk toward them.

"Polter*geist*!" shouted Resus as the trash can clattered past. "A type of ghost that can move things. They're known to have a bit of a temper!"

The vampire climbed out of the bush and ran on. Luke began to follow when a hand burst out of the soil and grabbed his ankle. A head appeared beside the hand: a head with cracked green skin, broken teeth, and dull eyes. Luke had played enough computer games to know what had hold of his leg.

It was a zombie.

Chapter Four
The Transformation

"**Resus!**" yelled Luke. His voice was swallowed up by the howling wind, and the vampire continued to run, unaware that he was now alone.

Luke turned back to try to free his leg. The hand that gripped it was covered in scabs and sores. Broken fingernails were blackened with dirt and dried blood. If he tried to pull free, he was likely to be scratched and possibly infected with some terrible disease.

Luke gazed into the zombie's milky eyes. The creature grinned at him, revealing a mouth crawling with worms and maggots. A cockroach scuttled out of a nostril and up into the zombie's left ear, dragging a trail of black snot behind it.

"Dude!" the zombie said. "What's the scoop?"

Luke stared at the hideous creature. Had it really spoken to him? Surely zombies were more interested in consuming your brain than engaging you in conversation?

"Excuse me?"

"Everything's, like, whizzing around, man!" continued the monster. "Caught me off guard and I totally lost my leg!"

"It's, er, a poltergeist attack," explained Luke. "They're known to have a bit of a temper, apparently."

"Poltergeist . . ." mused the zombie aloud. "Bogus, dude!"

"Absolutely!" agreed Luke, gesturing toward the creature's grip on his ankle. "But I'm afraid this is *my* leg, not yours."

 24

"No way!"

"Yes," said Luke. "Sorry."

Resus reappeared beside him. "I wondered where you'd gotten to."

"Busy meeting the locals," said Luke.

"What's the matter, Doug?" Resus asked.

"It's totally tripping me out, man!" replied the zombie. "The new dude here thinks this leg is his!"

"It is," said Resus. He peered through the bushes and spotted something wedged behind a garden gate. "I think *this* leg is yours," he added, retrieving the green-skinned limb.

"Far out, little vampire dude!" Doug beamed. The zombie released Luke's ankle and began to sink back into the ground. "Turf!" he yelled as the hole closed in over his greasy, matted hair. "I found it! Get the sewing kit, man!"

As Resus helped him to his feet, Luke made a mental note to be much kinder to computer-game zombies from now on.

The road widened into a square. Luke noticed there were other roads leading away from it: eight in total. Scream Street was shaped like a giant spider.

Standing proudly on one side of the square was a large shop: a brightly lit sign announced that this was Everwell's Emporium. Resus pushed open its silver doors and stepped inside. A bat tethered to a perch above the doorway let out a piercing squeal to announce the arrival of another customer.

Luke had barely followed him in when a shining sphere shot straight for his head, and he had to duck to avoid being hit. The fortune-teller's crystal ball shattered into a thousand pieces against the door frame. The shop was in chaos: glass bottles and colored gems soared around the ceiling as the poltergeist attack continued to grow in strength.

In the center of the shop stood a small figure wrapped in bandages from head to toe It gazed intently into a handheld mirror, ignoring the mayhem around it.

"Cleo?" said Resus. "What are you doing here?"

The girl shoved the mirror out of sight and rubbed furiously at a pink stain on the dressings around her mouth. "I, er, just came to see if Ecfa had finished putting her spell together!"

Resus stared at her. "Are you wearing lipstick?" he asked.

"Don't be ridiculous," replied Cleo, pulling bandages up from her chin to conceal the colorful blemish.

"You're a mummy!" Luke exclaimed.

"Not yet," replied the girl. "I'm much too young to have children!"

"No, I meant—"

"Just messing with you!" The mummy punched

27

him playfully on the arm. "I'm Cleo," she said. "You must be the new kid." The trio jumped as a shelving unit crashed to the floor behind them. "What a welcome to Scream Street this is!"

"He's a werewolf," announced Resus.

Cleo's eyes widened. "What, with all the claws and howling and stuff?"

Luke nodded.

"Cool!"

"Where's Eefa?" asked Resus.

"In here!" shouted a voice. Eefa Everwell appeared from a doorway at the back of the shop, protecting herself from flying objects with a circular tray. Luke blinked. *This* was a witch? Instead of the wart-covered hag he had imagined, Eefa Everwell was stunningly beautiful.

Pure white hair streaked with silver ran down her back. Her flawless skin was complemented by her dark violet lipstick and nail polish. Eyes the color of emeralds smiled at Luke.

Resus reached over and closed Luke's mouth. "Don't worry," he said, grinning. "Eefa has this effect on everyone. It's some kind of enchantment charm. You'll soon learn to ignore her."

Luke had just decided he wanted nothing

more than to stare at this vision of beauty for the rest of his life when a lamp shaped like a dragon bounced off his head, jolting him back to reality. Cleo grabbed his hand and dragged him behind the counter. Resus and Eefa joined them.

"Have you finished the spell, Eefa?" asked Cleo.

"Almost," the witch said, gesturing toward a scroll of parchment whirling around the center of the shop, "but it was pulled out of my hands when the attack started."

"I'll get it!" shouted Cleo. Before anyone could stop her, the mummy had climbed on top of the counter and jumped into the commotion beyond. A windchime crashed down from the ceiling, and she was forced to swerve to one side.

"Get back here!" yelled Resus.

Cleo stuck out her tongue at him as she snatched the parchment from the air. "Got it!" She grinned. She was running back to the safety of the counter when a jar of pulsing blue liquid smashed into a display of scented candles. The liquid sprayed over the candle flames, and a ball of fire exploded into the air.

Cleo was thrown back by the blast; she

smashed into the wall and collapsed beneath a large cotton wall hanging. The fire spread quickly. Luke leaped over the counter and pulled the burning wall hanging off the mummy, but it was too late. Cleo was on fire.

The mummy screamed as her bandages burned. Eefa grabbed a rug and began beating at the flames. "Resus!" she shrieked. "Get some water!"

Luke glanced up at the vampire. Resus was rooted to the spot, licking the tips of his fangs as he studied the flames, the fire reflected in his dark eyes.

Turning back to the blaze, Luke spotted a gap in the flames and dashed forward. Clutching Cleo's hand, he began to drag her away from the inferno. With a roar, the flames exploded, throwing him to the floor.

Luke jumped back to his feet, angrily rubbing at his scorched flesh. His eyes opened wide as a familiar feeling washed over him. His head swam, and everything slowed to a crawl inside his mind. He was starting to transform.

"Not now!" he pleaded aloud, but the change had already begun. Wolf fur spread across his

30

body like a thick blanket, and Luke gritted his teeth against the agony that was to come. To his amazement, nothing else happened. The transformation stopped after the fur was in place.

Luke discovered that his skin was now shielded from the heat of the fire, and he cautiously stepped into the flames. His clothes quickly burned away, but the dense fur protected his body. He lifted Cleo, then carried her out of the fire and laid her on the shop counter.

Eefa hurried to the mummy, raised her hands over her burned body, and started chanting under her breath. Cleo cried softly from the pain.

Then there was a sound like wind being sucked down a drain, and the bottles and jars still flying through the air fell to the floor with a smash. The poltergeist attack was over as quickly as it had started.

Luke tore a curtain from the window and wrapped it around himself as the thick strands of fur retracted into his skin. Within seconds he was human again.

Resus crunched over to him through the broken glass. "That was amazing!" he said. "I just froze, but you were great. How did you do that?"

"I don't know," replied Luke. "I didn't change completely."

Eefa looked up from the spell she was working over Cleo. "You're in Scream Street," she said. "Werewolves have lived here before, and they all experienced partial transformations of some kind or another."

Resus clapped Luke on the back. "I take back what I said earlier." He beamed. "You're anything but a normal."

Luke allowed himself a smile. Perhaps living in Scream Street wouldn't be so bad after all. . . .

His thoughts were interrupted by the screech of the bat as the door opened. Bella Negative appeared, a serious expression on her face.

"Luke," she said. "It's your mom."

Chapter Five
The Landlord

Back in the kitchen of 13 Scream Street, Luke watched as Bella Negative bandaged his mom's broken arm.

"We were hiding beneath the table when the iron stove flew over and hit your mom," said Alston. "There was nothing we could do."

"What about magic?" asked Luke. "Eefa was helping Cleo at the shop."

"Eefa was just easing Cleo's pain," said Bella. "Injuries have to heal naturally here, just like in your world."

"*My* world!" snapped Luke. "None of this would have happened if we had just been left alone in 'my world'!"

"This is your world now," said Bella. "You're a werewolf; you belong here."

"My mom and dad don't belong here, though, do they?" shouted Luke. He spun around. "Look at them! They're terrified."

"Luke," said Mr. Watson. "It's OK . . ."

"No, Dad, it's not OK," said Luke. "This is all my fault—you're here because of me! I'm taking you home."

"That's impossible," said Alston, "unless you're Samuel Skipstone."

"Who?"

"Samuel Skipstone wrote a book about Scream Street," explained Bella. "Legend says he discovered the only way out."

"Then I'll read that!" said Luke.

"It's nothing but a fairy tale," insisted Alston. "Once you've been brought to Scream Street, you're here to stay."

"That's ridiculous!" shouted Luke. "There must be a way out. We can't—"

The front door smashed open, and a large, sweating man appeared in the kitchen doorway, puffing at a thick cigar. Foul smoke filled the air around him.

"Sir Otto!" said Alston.

"Why are all the lights on in this house?" roared the man, stroking a silk scarf that covered his neck. "You're wasting gas!"

"We've been clearing up after the poltergeist attack," explained Bella. "This family has just arrived, and Mrs. Watson has broken her arm."

The man opened his mouth to reply but stopped when a tall, thin figure with lank red hair entered the room. "I don't get it, Uncle Otto," he said.

"How many times do I have to tell you, Dixon?" the man growled. "When we're out in public, you are to refer to me as *Sir*."

"Sorry, Sir Uncle Otto." Dixon smiled. "I just don't understand why you got me to kick down the door when there are people inside. We could have knocked!"

Sir Otto slapped his nephew across the head. "Idiot!" Regaining his composure, he turned back to Bella. "You know the rules! Only one light to be burning at a time. No exceptions!"

Sir Otto pulled the cigar out of his mouth and smiled nastily at Luke. "Hello, little freak," he purred. "I'm Sir Otto Sneer, your new landlord." Then he turned to his nephew. "Dixon," he roared, jamming the cigar back between his lips. "Disconnect them!"

"You can't!" shouted Alston. "They need gas!"

"Then they should have obeyed the rules," snarled the landlord as he disappeared out into the street. Within minutes, the house was plunged into darkness. The only sound was of Mrs. Watson sobbing.

"I've got to take my mom and dad home," muttered Luke.

Bella appeared beside him. "There might be a way," she whispered. "But you'll have to do some work first."

"What kind of work?" asked Luke.

"Schoolwork!"

"And, of course, a very warm welcome to our newest student!"

Luke stared at his new teacher—or, rather, *through* his new teacher. Dr. Skully was a skeleton. "I spent a long career as a laboratory skeleton," he had explained earlier. "Now retired, I devote my life to teaching others."

Luke was sitting with Resus and Cleo in Dr. Skully's dining room, set up as a classroom, complete with desks, a blackboard, and bookshelves.

"Cookie, anyone?" asked the teacher's skeletal wife as she entered with a tray of hot drinks and snacks.

"Really, Tibia," scolded the teacher lightly. "How many times must I ask you not to simply barge in without—Oh, my, are those chocolate chip?"

Luke took the opportunity to lean across and whisper to Resus, "This is all very cozy, but how does it help me get my parents home?"

"My mom said there's a book that shows how to open a doorway to your world," replied the vampire. *"Skipstone's Tales of Scream Street."*

"Skipstone?" said Cleo. "The man who claimed the Loch Ness Monster lived in his toilet bowl? Everyone knows his stories are crazy!"

Resus shrugged. "Even the weirdest nursery rhyme has some truth in it."

"OK," said Cleo, "it's worth a try. But how do we find the book?"

"What do you mean 'we'?" hissed Luke. "I'm doing this alone."

"No, you're not!" said Cleo. "I lay in silence for centuries while explorers searched my tomb. Now there's an adventure on my doorstep, and I'm not missing it!"

"You can count me in too!" Resus grinned.

Luke was surprised to feel relieved. He had no idea what might be involved in opening this doorway, and any help he could get would be welcome.

"Right!" said Dr. Skully as he munched on a cookie. The crumbs bounced off his rib cage as they fell to the floor. "Math books open to chapter—"

"Could you tell us about Samuel Skipstone, please, sir?" interrupted Resus.

"Skipstone?" said the teacher. "School is a place for facts, Master Negative, not the exploration of fictitious ramblings!" The skeleton shook his head. "Today we are here to study mathematics."

Luke sighed as Dr. Skully turned to the blackboard to write out a complicated algebra equation. "What do we do now?"

"Find the book ourselves," replied Resus. "If anyone's got a copy, it will be Dr. Skully. We just need to search these bookcases."

"But how do we get him out of the room?" hissed Cleo.

Resus winked. "Leave it to me!" He reached inside his cloak and pulled out a large bone, rotting shreds of meat still attached.

"Where did you get that?" asked Luke.

"You can thank my granddad," replied Resus.

"He gave you that leg bone?" said Luke.

"This *is* his leg bone!" The vampire grinned.

"You're disgusting," moaned Cleo.

"Why?" said Resus. "He doesn't need it; he's been dead for years! Now, check this out. . . ."

 41

He waggled the bone beneath the desk. "Scapula, here, boy!"

A skeleton dog padded into the room and took the bone in its teeth. It trotted through the open back door and out to a hole in the garden. Suddenly the dog seemed to become confused, and after looking from the bone to its own skeletal body and back again, it jumped into the hole and covered itself with soil.

"Dr. Skully," called Resus, "Scapula's burying himself in the garden again."

"Oh, dear!" groaned the teacher, running from the room.

Resus leaped to his feet. "Right, we've got about two minutes!" he said. "We're looking for *Skipstone's Tales of Scream Street.*"

Luke began to search. The teacher's shelves featured titles such as *Dragon Wrangling, In Touch with the Spirits,* and *101 Ways to Clean Up After a Bog Monster,* but there was no sign of *Skipstone's Tales of Scream Street.* "This is hopeless!" he moaned.

"It's got to be here somewhere," said Resus. "Try the top shelf."

"I'll do it," said Cleo, dragging a desk across the room and climbing onto it.

"Is it up there?" Luke asked.

"Is WHAT up there?" boomed a voice behind them. The trio spun around to find Dr. Skully standing in the doorway. Scapula sat at his feet.

"*Skipstone's Tales of Scream Street,* sir," admitted Cleo, climbing down.

"And why would it be up there?" asked the teacher. "Especially when I have explained that Skipstone's writings are worth little, if anything, to the reader?"

"It's Luke, sir!" said Resus. "He's turning into a werewolf again! We were hoping there would be something in the book that would help him."

Dr. Skully turned to Luke. "Is this true?" he asked. "Are you in the early stages of your transformation?"

Luke swallowed hard. "Yes, sir," he lied feebly, waving his arms around a little and pretending to growl. "Grrrr!"

The skeleton sighed. "Well, although there is no way to reverse a werewolf transformation,

Samuel Skipstone did, apparently, research the subject."

Luke's eyes lit up. "Do you have a copy of his book, sir?" he asked.

"I own the *only* copy," replied the teacher.

"Can we see it?" asked Cleo.

"Unfortunately not," said Dr. Skully, shaking his head. "It was confiscated."

"Confiscated?" said Luke. "Who confiscates a book from a teacher?"

Chapter Six
The Hellhounds

"Sir Otto Sneer?" asked Luke as he, Resus, and Cleo arrived at the gates of a sprawling mansion opposite Everwell's Emporium. A sign read: SNEER HALL.

"The nice man who disconnected your gas supply," said Resus.

"And *he* confiscated *Skipstone's Tales of Scream Street?*"

"He confiscates everything," said Cleo. "Spells, potions, souvenirs. I had a pet hamster until he decided it was against the rules!"

"He does it to keep us in our place," said Resus. "Whenever he thinks we're satisfied with life, he just takes stuff from us, or rations it out."

"Like the gas?" asked Luke.

Resus nodded. "My dad says we used to have electricity, too."

"Did he confiscate the sun as well?" said Luke, looking up as a blanket of dark clouds rolled in to obscure the stars. "We're supposed to be on our lunch break, but it looks like the middle of the night!"

Resus grinned. "I guess that living in constant night will take a bit of getting used to!"

"Why would Sir Otto want the book?" asked Cleo.

Resus tried the gates; they were locked. "I've got no idea, but I don't think he'll be too happy that we've come to ask about it."

Cleo reached up and pulled the bell cord. A window in the mansion flung open with a crash, and the landlord appeared, cigar jutting from his mouth.

46

"What?" he roared.

"Mr. Sneer, it's Cleo Farr—"

"SIR Sneer!" thundered the landlord.

"Sorry," said Cleo. "*Sir* Sneer. We were hoping we might be able to take a quick peek at the book you, er . . . borrowed from Dr. Skully recently."

"Who is it?" roared a voice in the background. Luke stared as the face of Sir Otto began to change. The skin pulled tighter, and long red hair sprouted from the landlord's scalp. Within seconds, Dixon was smiling down at them.

"Fooled you!" He giggled, waving. "It was me all the time!"

"Dixon is Sir Otto's nephew," whispered Resus. "He's a shapeshifter, but not exactly the sharpest fang in the mouth, if you know what I mean!"

Dixon was shoved roughly aside as the real Sir Otto appeared at the window. "Which book are you talking about?" he demanded.

"*Skipstone's Tales of Scream Street,* sir," said Luke. "Can we see it?"

"Certainly not!" bellowed the landlord. "How dare you freaks expect decent, normal people to

47

share their belongings with the likes of you?" Sir Otto slammed the window and disappeared from view.

"No!" yelled Luke, reaching for the bell again.

Cleo grabbed his arm. "It's no good," she said. "He won't listen."

"But we have to read that book!" said Luke.

"And we will." Resus smiled. "But there's more than one way. . . ." He reached inside his cloak and produced a can of beer.

"I don't know what the law is here in Scream Street," said Luke, "but in my world, we're much too young to drink."

"It's not for *us,*" said Resus, crouching on the grass beside the path and pulling back the can's pulltop. It opened with a *tshh!* and, almost instantly, a hand with cracked green skin shot out of the soil beneath his feet and grabbed it.

"Brewski!" The zombie's beaming face appeared. "Cheers, little dude!"

"Doug," said Resus. "We need a favor."

Luke followed the zombie through the tunnel he had dug out for them, delighted that Resus had

48

found a way to get inside the mansion and, at the same time, terrified that the earth would collapse around them at any moment.

"Are you sure you little dudes want to visit this place?" asked Doug from the front of the line. "I heard there's some heavy stuff that goes on in there!"

"We have to," replied Resus. "Sir Otto's got a book we need to look at."

"Well, if it's for the cause of literature." Doug beamed, satisfied. "You know, I wrote a book once."

Luke smiled. "Amazing," he said. "And I thought zombies were all about killing people and eating brains. What was the book called?"

"Top Ten Ways to Cook Human Flesh."

Resus fought back a laugh as he heard Luke catch his breath.

Doug reached up and burst through the roof of the tunnel. Fresh air flooded Luke's nostrils as the zombie helped him to climb out next to a side door to Sneer Hall.

"Thanks for your help," said Resus.

"Anytime, dudes!" The zombie grinned. "Always happy to stick it to the man!" And with a wink, he disappeared into the hole, dragging earth over himself.

Resus turned to the door. "Time for a little breaking and entering," he said. He slid a long fingernail into the lock of the door and wiggled it around.

"Will that work?" asked Luke.

"Strong enough to cut glass." Resus grinned. "You just have to be careful not to forget about them and scratch your bum."

With a soft click, the lock released. Resus gripped the handle. "I hope the alarm's not on." He pulled open the door. Silence. "I think we're safe," he said. Then the vampire's smile faltered as a deep-throated growl rang out behind them.

Luke spun around to discover two large black dogs running their way. Fire flickered in their eyes, and saliva dripped from their mouths, burning the ground with a hiss. "What," he said, his eyes wide, "are *they*?"

"Hellhounds!" screamed Cleo.

"Quick!" yelled Resus. "Inside!" He pulled Luke and Cleo through the door and slammed it behind them. They were plunged into darkness.

"Where are we?" whispered Cleo.

Luke felt around, knocking over a wooden pole. "I don't know."

The gloom was pierced by the beam of a flashlight. Resus waved the light. "Look what I found in my pocket," he said.

"I've got to get one of those cloaks," said Cleo.

In the dim light, Luke realized that they were in a small storage shed filled with gardening equipment. The pole he had knocked over was a rake. "This isn't an entrance to the house at all!" he moaned.

The door shook as one of the dogs threw itself at it from the other side. "That lock won't hold out for long," said Cleo. The door rattled again.

"They're not going to give up," said Luke. "What do we do?"

"Can't you transform into your werewolf self and fight them off?" asked Resus.

Luke shook his head. "It doesn't work like that. I'd need to be angry and—"

Without a word, Resus swung the flashlight around and hit him across the head.

"Ow!" yelled Luke. "What did you do that for?"

"I'm trying to make you angry!" said Resus.

"Is this some sort of joke to you?" snapped Luke.

"Of course not," said Resus. "Chill out."

"Chill out?" demanded Luke. "You're trying to change me into the creature that brought my parents here, and you want me to chill out?"

"Luke, I'm sure he didn't mean—" began Cleo.

"Why don't *you* bite them?" interrupted Luke. "You're the scary vampire!"

"Please!" begged Cleo. There was another thud as the dogs attacked the door.

"'I'll only bite you if you annoy me,' you said. Well, I'm annoying you now, Resus, so either bite me or get out there and bite those dogs!"

"Stop it!" shouted Cleo, grabbing his arm.

Luke shook himself free. "I'll tell you why you're not going to fight those hellhounds," he roared. "It's because you're a coward!"

"No!" yelled Resus. "It's because I'm a normal!"

Luke stared at Resus. "That's not true," he said. "You're a vampire. Your parents . . . I've seen them. They're vampires!"

Resus wiped his eyes with his cape, smearing the dark rings around them. It was makeup. "My parents *are* vampires," he said. "I'm some sort of genetic freak. Born with blond hair, you can see my reflection in mirrors . . . and the only thing that happens to me in the sunlight is that I get a tan."

"But—your nails!" said Luke. "You picked the lock with your fingernails!"

Resus held up his hand and showed Luke where the metal fingernails fitted over his own.

"Fake," he said. "Just like these." He reached into his mouth, unclipped his fangs, and took them out.

"I—I didn't know," said Luke.

"I try to be scary," said Resus quietly. "I try to act threatening so that people won't know the truth, but it's no use. I'm not a real vampire at all!"

The hellhounds continued to throw themselves at the door.

"Then there's only one way out," said Luke, picking up the rake. "We fight."

Chapter Seven
The Library

The door burst open, hitting one of the hellhounds and knocking it off balance. Luke leaped out, twirling the rake as if it were a staff. He swung it around, catching the legs of the other dog and sending it tumbling.

Resus followed, wielding a shovel, which he brought down on the first dog's head as it staggered to its feet. It crumpled back to the ground, whining.

The second hellhound yowled, fire raging in its eyes. It lunged for Resus, but Cleo jumped into its way and knocked it to one side with a metal trash can lid. The trio stood firm, makeshift weapons raised, as the hellhounds shook their heads and snarled.

"If we can push them back, we might be able to get around to the main doors," said Luke.

"We'd better hope they're not locked," said Resus, "or we'll be just as trapped there."

Luke nodded. "One of us should go and find a way in while the other two keep these things occupied."

"I'll do it!" shouted Cleo, dropping her trash-can lid and running off.

Resus grabbed for her bandages, but she was moving too fast. "She never learns!" he groaned. He snatched the trash can lid from the ground and used it to hold the dogs at bay.

The two hellhounds split up, then advanced from either side, forcing Luke and Resus to stand back-to-back. One of the hounds darted for Luke, teeth bared. Luke swung the rake around, catching the dog in the throat.

Its companion howled with rage and leaped forward. Its front paws shoved Luke to the ground. The dog scraped a claw across Luke's face, drawing blood. Luke tried to hit it with the rake, but his arms were trapped beneath the hellhound's back legs. He was pinned down.

The dog growled down at Luke, deadly saliva threatening to drip into his eyes at any moment. As it lunged for his throat, Resus swung the trash can lid at the creature's face. The dog fell to the grass, howling with pain.

"Thanks," said Luke as Resus helped him to his feet.

"Any time," replied the vampire, keeping his eyes on the dogs as they approached again. One of the hellhounds reared up onto its back legs, and Resus was forced to hold the trash can lid out like a shield to protect himself.

The dog dropped down, spotting the reflection of Cleo running for the doors in the shiny metal lid. Barking a warning, it turned and raced after the fleeing mummy, its companion following.

"Cleo!" bellowed Luke.

Cleo turned to see the dogs on her tail and picked up speed, her feet pounding against the grass as she ran. She could hear the growling of the hellhounds as they got closer, and she fixed her gaze on the doors ahead. She had to reach them. Had to get inside.

The first dog pounced and landed squarely on Cleo's back, pushing her to the ground and ripping at her bandages. The second dog grabbed her foot between its teeth and bit down.

Cleo screamed as acidic saliva burned into her skin. She tried to crawl away, but the dogs pulled her back, nipping and scratching at her, toying with their prey before they destroyed it.

Luke and Resus ran as fast as they could toward the mummy, knowing they had only seconds to save her from the rabid hounds.

Luke raised the rake into the air and brought it down hard onto the dog at Cleo's throat. It yelped as the metal prongs pierced its flesh. Resus hit it with his shovel, and the dog collapsed to one side, unconscious.

The second dog pulled back its lips and snarled angrily at the boys. Resus snorted back a laugh. "You're not the only one with teeth!" he shouted.

The young vampire turned his eyes upward until only the whites were visible. He opened his mouth wide, licked the tips of his fake fangs, and hissed. The hellhound yelped in terror and raced away across the flower beds.

 59

Luke dropped to his knees beside Cleo. Her bandages were ripped and burned by the dog's drool. She wasn't moving.

Cleo opened her eyes. She was lying on a plush couch in a room built of iron and glass. Plants filled every available space.

A face appeared among the foliage: Resus. "Morning, sleepy!" he joked.

Cleo sat up, wincing as a throbbing sensation filled her skull. She touched a tender lump on her forehead.

"You hit your head on a rock when the dog pounced," explained Resus. "Knocked yourself out cold. We thought it was a lot worse for a moment, though."

Cleo looked down at her bandages. Some of them were missing and had been replaced with strips of silky red material. "What happened?" she asked.

"Your bandages were covered with that acid the dogs were drooling. We had to get them off before they burned your skin too badly."

Cleo ran her fingers over the red material. "Wait, this is the lining of your cape," she said.

 60

Resus shrugged. "What do I need it for? Only real vampires have capes."

Cleo scowled. "You *are* a real vampire, Resus!"

"He certainly is," said Luke, pushing his way through a small jungle of plant life. "You should have seen the way he scared off that hellhound!"

Cleo stood, testing her leg. It ached when she put any pressure on it, but at least she was able to walk. "Where are we?" she asked.

"Sir Otto's conservatory," said Luke. "The front doors were locked, but we found an open window here. It wasn't easy getting you through it. Have you ever thought about going on a diet?" Cleo slapped him playfully on the arm.

"Did you find anything?" asked Resus.

"No sign of the book yet," replied Luke, "but there is something rather interesting out in the hallway. . . ."

Luke, Resus, and Cleo gazed up at a portrait of a vampire.

"That," said Luke, "looks like you!"

"It does," agreed Cleo.

"It's my ancestor," explained Resus. "Count Negatov."

"Wasn't he one of the first residents of Scream Street?" asked Cleo.

Resus nodded. "He was forced out of Transylvania and came here to build Scream Street, along with the other founding fathers. My dad told me about him."

"Sounds like your family and Sir Otto's go back a long way." Luke grinned. "You sure you can't just go up —"

"Someone's coming!" hissed Cleo, quickly pulling Luke and Resus into a gap behind a near-by sideboard. Sir Otto's nephew, Dixon, appeared at the end of the corridor, singing to himself: *"You put your left arm in, your left arm out . . ."*

"He's coming this way!" said Cleo.

Luke searched for a better hiding place. There was a doorway opposite, but no way of crossing to it without being spotted. They needed a diversion.

Dixon paused to make faces at himself in a mirror, and Luke saw his chance. He grabbed a vase from the sideboard and hurled it along the corridor. It soared through the air over Dixon's head and hit a suit of armor.

The armor swayed to one side and then

back again, crashing down on top of Dixon. He screamed. "Help! It's attacking me! Help!"

Luke darted across the hall and opened the door. He, Resus, and Cleo hurried inside, closing it behind them. They found themselves in a richly decorated room lined with bookshelves.

"I guess this is the library," said Resus.

"Well," said Luke, "if the book's anywhere, it will be in here."

"Right," said Resus. "Let's start searching."

"Not again!" moaned Cleo. "We'll be here all ni—"

The door to the library crashed open, and Dixon entered, his arms piled high with pieces of armor. "I'm telling you, Uncle Otto, it jumped on top of me!"

Luke and Resus ducked under a large desk as Cleo dropped to the floor and slid beneath a leather couch.

Sir Otto entered the room behind Dixon, cigar clamped firmly between his lips. "Jumped on top of you, indeed! You're a waste of DNA!"

Resus nudged Luke and pointed to a silver-backed book the landlord was carrying. "That's it," he mouthed. "*Skipstone's Tales of Scream Street!*"

Dixon dropped the armor onto the floor with a clatter.

"Be careful!" roared the landlord. "That armor is centuries old."

"You should get new stuff, then, Uncle Otto," said Dixon. "Something with silver sequins— or purple, to match your face when you get angry!"

"Don't be cheeky!"

Sir Otto waddled over to one of the shelves and pulled a book out of its place. There was a click and a whirr as a doorway in the shelves slid open. The landlord disappeared through it. Dixon remained in the library.

"How's it going with the book, Uncle?" he called.

"It's not!" said the landlord. "The stupid thing still hasn't told me anything."

"Do you want me to try?" asked Dixon. "I like books!"

Sir Otto reappeared without the book, the doorway closing behind him. "The only books you can cope with are the kind you have to color in," he sneered.

"That's not fair!" Dixon's lower lip trembled

 64

as he followed his uncle out of the library. "I like comics, too!"

As the door closed, Luke, Resus, and Cleo climbed to their feet.

"We have to get into that secret room," said Luke. "Then we can find out what Samuel Skipstone wrote about how to leave Scream Street."

Chapter Eight
The Book

Luke pulled out book after book, trying to remember which title Sir Otto had moved to trigger the secret door. He reached the end of the shelf, but nothing had happened.

"This is ridiculous!" he snapped. "I know it was one of these!" He kicked out angrily, stubbing his toe against the shelves. Pain shot through his foot, and he dropped onto a nearby couch to pull off his sneaker and massage the injured toe.

"That hurtsh!" he hissed.

"Hurtsh?" repeated Resus. "Have your lips stopped working?"

Luke shrugged. "It jusht came out like —"

Another bolt of pain hit him, this time shooting through his face as his upper jaw splintered and pushed outward to create a wolf's snout. A long tongue lolled out of his mouth, and thick whiskers sprouted from either side of his nose.

"Oh, thish ish jusht fantashtic!" he moaned, running his fingers over the length of his doglike features.

"You sound just like me when I first got these clip-on fangs!" Resus giggled.

"That shkunk inshide your cloak ish decomposhing fasht," grumbled Luke, sniffing at the air with his new, sensitive nose. He smiled as another scent filled his nostrils. "I can shmell Shir Shneer!"

Cleo shook her head. "Nope," she said, "didn't get a word of that!"

"Otto Shneer!" said Luke, wiping strings of drool from his chin. "I've picked up hish schent!"

"Oh!" exclaimed Cleo. "I can smell him too; those cigars really stink."

"It'sh not the shigarsh I can shmell," said Luke, slavering. "I can shee the booksh he wash touch-ing!" He sniffed the row of books, following the landlord's scent.

"Thish one," he announced. "And hish fing-ersh only touched the firsht two shentimetres." He carefully pulled the book out a short way. There was a click, and the unit slid inward to reveal a dark passageway beyond.

Resus grinned. "Shuper-duper!"

Luke's face shrank back as he led the way down a stone staircase.

"Doesn't that hurt?" asked Cleo.

"Like you wouldn't believe," replied Luke. "But it's proving helpful."

"We need a little light on the situation," said Resus. He reached inside his cloak and pulled out a length of wood that crackled with fire at one end.

Cleo stared. "Why would you have a flaming torch inside your cloak?"

Resus shrugged. "I lost the battery-operated one fighting the hellhounds."

 68

In the flickering light, Luke, Resus, and Cleo examined Sir Otto's secret room. Both the walls and the floor were of simple, bare stone. A series of wires and metal clamps pushed through one of the walls.

"What are these?" asked Cleo, studying a vice that jutted out.

"I have no idea," said Resus. "But I know what that is!" Following his gaze, Luke and Cleo saw *Skipstone's Tales of Scream Street* sitting on top of a stone pillar.

Luke reached out to take it, but as his hand touched the book, it was surrounded by a ball of white light. He yelped and pulled his fingers back.

"What's the matter?" asked Resus.

"It gave me a shock!" exclaimed Luke, sucking his fingertips.

Resus smiled. "I'll get it," he said. Within seconds the vampire was also nursing a jolted hand as the ball of light wrapped itself around the book again.

"I haven't come this far to walk away now," said Luke, reaching out with his other hand. There was a crackle, and he spun away, cursing.

Resus tried again with his uninjured hand. Soon both boys were hopping round the room, fingers jammed into their armpits.

"Are you both brain-dead?" Cleo asked. "It's obviously some sort of energy shield. Whenever you reach out for the book, the shield activates and zaps you."

"And what do you suggest we do about it?" asked Luke.

"Leave it to mummy!" Cleo grinned. She unwrapped the bandages from her right arm. The skin beneath was black and wrinkled, like that of burned chicken. She reached out and grabbed hold of the book. The energy shield fizzed into life, and Cleo gritted her teeth against the pain as she lifted the tome off its pillar.

"Boys!" she said.

School had finished for the day, and Luke, Resus, and Cleo now sat on the floor in Resus's bedroom. The book lay on the carpet between them, the face of a man raised up from its silver cover.

A variety of fierce-looking weapons were hung by lengths of wire from the ceiling above them, and on the pillow of Resus's bed was a teddy in a cape. Its head was missing. The walls were splashed with what Luke hoped was red paint.

"What do we do now?" asked Cleo.

"We read," said Luke. He grabbed the book and opened it to a random page. It showed a recipe for gnome stew. The following page advertised disguise kits for germs, while the next was

71

taken up with a rousing poem about toenails. Everything was written in the same scrawled handwriting.

A feeling of hopelessness began to wash over Luke as he flicked faster and faster through the pages. The book had absolutely nothing in it that could help him open a doorway home. Luke threw it to the floor.

"We went through all that and the book's useless!" he moaned.

"I wouldn't say useless. . . ." said a voice. Luke glanced up at Resus and Cleo, but neither of them had spoken. Cautiously he turned the book over.

The face on the cover now had its eyes open, and it was smiling. "Thank you. I have a dust allergy, and this carpet hasn't been vacuumed for a while."

"We don't have any electricity," said Resus slowly, not quite certain if he should be talking to a book. "We have to rely on the spiders to clean up."

"Ah yes, the electricity," said the face. "I know all about that."

"Excuse me," said Cleo, "but who *are* you?"

The silver face grinned. "Where are my

manners?" it exclaimed. "Samuel Skipstone—
author of *Skipstone's Tales of Scream Street*!"

"You wrote this book?" asked Luke.

"Wrote the book?" Skipstone beamed. "I *am*
the book!" He gazed at the surprised faces around
him, then sighed.

"This bit always confuses people," he said.
"Most authors write their books and then their
involvement ends. But I was so engrossed in my
work that as I lay dying, I used a spell to merge
my spirit with the pages."

"So you're trapped in there?" asked Cleo.

"Trapped?" replied Skipstone. "Not at all! I am here by choice!"

"But the pages, I mean *your* pages, are filled with silly things like poems and sketches," said Resus. "There's nothing serious about Scream Street in it at all."

Samuel Skipstone winked. "What better place to hide important knowledge than among useless claptrap? I do not discuss my work with just anyone."

"So you haven't told Sir Otto what you know?" asked Luke.

"Nor will I," answered Skipstone. "I do not approve of Sneer's plans for Scream Street. I have remained mute at his every question."

"I heard Sir Otto say you hadn't told him anything," said Luke. "I thought he just hadn't found what he was looking for, but he must have meant you weren't speaking!"

Skipstone nodded. "However, for three such eager young minds, I am prepared to talk. Ask and I shall answer!"

Luke took a deep breath. "I want to leave Scream Street."

74

Samuel Skipstone fixed Luke with his silvery eyes. "And why would a werewolf want to leave the place where he can live among those who accept him?"

Cleo gasped. "You can tell that Luke is a werewolf?"

"I am something of an expert on the subject of lycanthropy," said the author. "There are ways of knowing a werewolf when you see one."

"It's not for me," continued Luke. "It's for my mom and dad." He told Samuel Skipstone about how his family had arrived in Scream Street. He explained how scared his parents were and how, even though he had made friends here, he didn't want to put his parents through the ordeal any longer.

When Luke had finished speaking, Skipstone remained quiet for a moment, then spoke softly. "It is a noble quest to leave the place where you belong for the sake of those you love. I will help all I can."

"You'll tell me how to take my parents home?" exclaimed Luke.

 75

"It is not that simple," replied Skipstone. "Only the six founding fathers of Scream Street have the power to make such a thing possible."

"Founding fathers?" said Cleo. "Like Count Negatov?"

"Indeed," said Skipstone. "Allow me to introduce them. . . ."

Chapter Nine
The Clue

The silver book flicked open to a page containing an article about basic gargoyle maintenance. Luke, Resus, and Cleo watched as the handwritten words faded away and an illustration took their place.

The picture showed a street party with figures sitting around a long table, eating and laughing. As Luke watched, the image began to move. There was no sound except the scratch of pencil on paper as the illustration was constantly redrawn, but it was obvious that everyone was having a great deal of fun.

"That's Scream Street!" he said.

"It can't be," said Cleo. "The sun's out!"

"The sun used to shine every day," explained Skipstone. "It is only recently that the sky has been veiled in darkness."

A vampire stood at the head of the table and raised a glass. "Count Negatov!" exclaimed Resus. "The first vampire in Scream Street!"

"These are the founding fathers and their families," said the author.

"What are they celebrating?" asked Cleo as the vampire's silent toast was greeted with equally noise-free applause.

"The completion of Scream Street," said Skipstone. "The electricity generator had just been put in place. No longer would the residents have to cook and heat their homes with dangerous gas."

Resus glanced up at the flickering flame that

barely lit his bedroom. "Doesn't look like we've come very far," he commented.

The picture faded, and the scrawled article came back into view. "The founding fathers can give you the power to see your greatest wish realized," said Skipstone.

"You mean like opening a doorway back to my world?" asked Luke.

"If that is your desire, then yes," said the author.

"But surely everyone in that picture is long gone," said Cleo.

"Very true," replied Skipstone.

Luke's heart sank. "Then we're stuck here!"

"Do not dismiss the founding fathers so quickly," said Skipstone. "They all left behind something to help those who came after."

"What do you mean?" asked Cleo.

"They each donated something very personal," said the author. "Once collected, these relics will provide the finder with their combined power."

"What's a relic?" asked Cleo.

"It's like a souvenir," explained Resus. "Something you use to remember something or someone."

Cleo smiled. "So all we have to do is find these six relics and Luke can open a doorway home?" she asked. "That doesn't sound too hard."

"It might not be that simple," answered Skipstone. "The relics are hidden well, and only clues were left to their true locations. They must also be collected in the exact order in which they were donated."

"It can't be impossible, though," said Luke. "They were left behind to help people. To give them the power of the founding fathers."

"Indeed," said the author. "However, they could easily be misused. You must ensure that the relics do not fall into the wrong hands."

"You mean . . ."

Samuel Skipstone's voice was solemn. "Sir Otto Sneer! I would imagine that his plans for this community are very dark indeed. If he regains possession of me, your family will never leave Scream Street."

"I'll be careful," promised Luke.

Skipstone smiled. "Then allow me to reveal the location of the first relic."

The book flipped open once more. Spidery

handwriting dissolved from the page, revealing a hidden portion of text:

In the tunnel, through the slime,
the vampire lies for all of time;
down where all is constant night,
the source of power here will bite.

"There's only one kind of slimy tunnel around here," said Resus. "The sewer. There's a trap-door in our cellar that leads down there."

"Then that's where we're going," said Luke. "Do we need to—"

"Which one of you freaks stole my book?"

Sir Otto's voice echoed along Scream Street. Luke, Resus, and Cleo dashed to the window. They could just see the landlord standing in the central square, Dixon at his side.

"I guess he's figured out he's one talking book short," said Resus.

Sir Otto bit down hard on his cigar and stroked the silk scarf at his neck. *"I know you monsters stick together,"* he roared, *"but if one of you has the guts*

to come out and tell me who has my book, you shall
be spared!"

"Spared from what?" asked Cleo.

"I don't know," replied Resus, "but I don't
like the look of *that*."

As the trio watched, Dixon uncoiled a length
of wire from the gates of Sneer Hall and attached
it to a plunger at Sir Otto's feet.

"You have until the count of ten!" yelled the landlord. "Ten, nine, eight . . ."

"It's a bomb!" whispered Cleo.

Luke shook his head. "I don't think so. That wire leads back into Sneer Hall. He wouldn't blow up his own mansion."

". . . three, two, one!" Sir Otto gripped the handle of the plunger. "Don't say I didn't warn you, Scream Street!" He pushed down hard. Instantly there was a rush of wind, and objects began to fly around Resus's bedroom.

Cleo jumped to avoid a falling ax as the wires tethering it to the ceiling snapped. "It's a poltergeist attack!" she said. "He's started another attack!"

"That's impossible," said Resus. "You can't control poltergeists!"

"Sneer's obviously found a way," said Luke. "I need to get to my mom and dad, make sure they're OK this time."

Resus grabbed his arm. "Are you crazy? If you go out there, the book will be torn from your hands by the poltergeist! Sir Otto will have it back in no time."

"So what do we do?"

83

"We start searching for the relics right now," said Resus. "The sooner your parents are away from all of this, the better."

As Luke and Resus made for the bedroom door, a squeal and a thump from behind stopped them in their tracks. The boys turned. Cleo was lying on the floor, a sword that had been hanging from the ceiling buried deep in her chest.

"Cleo!" shouted Resus, kneeling beside her.

The mummy's eyes flickered open. "That stings," she moaned, reaching up to pull the blade from her rib cage.

"Stings?" said Luke. "You should be dead! It went right through your heart!"

"I don't think so," said Cleo, handing the sword to Resus and rearranging her bandages to cover the hole. "My heart is in a golden casket in my bedroom."

"What?" exclaimed Luke. "How?"

"I'm a mummy!" said Cleo. "We have our internal organs removed before we're buried in our tombs. Didn't you have history at school?"

Standing, she stretched to ease the discomfort of the wound, then headed for the door. "Well?" she said. "Are we going down to the sewers, or not?"

Before either boy could reply, Cleo had left the room.

Resus pulled open the trapdoor and thrust the flaming torch into the hole. Luke was just able to make out the ground below. "You're sure this is it?"

"It's the only slime-coated tunnel I know of." Resus climbed down the short ladder and landed in a puddle with a splash. Luke followed.

"I'm going to have to find a new bandage supplier now I've met you," groaned Cleo as she joined them in the mud.

"I'll send you a box once I've opened a doorway home." Luke grinned. "Now, which way do we go?" He looked up and down the sewer tunnel.

"If I was hunting for a vampire, I'd go as deep as possible," said Resus.

"Down it is, then," said Luke, leading the way into the darkness. At each junction, Luke, Resus, and Cleo followed the tunnel that led deeper belowground.

After a while they found themselves in a vast underground cavern. Green moss clung to the walls and gave off an eerie glow.

"Gutweed," explained Resus, tucking the torch back inside his cloak. "They used to use it to light children's bedrooms at night."

"I can't imagine sleeping with that stuff in my room," said Luke. "It stinks!"

There was a crash as Cleo knocked something over in the dim light. She reached down and picked up a piece of broken dinner plate. "What's this doing here?" she asked.

The trio explored the cavern. Piles of books, clothing, toys, and more lay around. Thousands of household objects were stacked from floor to ceiling, the luminous gutweed clinging to everything.

"This is all the stuff Sir Otto's confiscated over the years!" said Resus.

"Well, it's probably ruined now," said Luke. "It'll stink after spending so much time down here. I'm not sure I'll be able to get rid of the stench myself!"

"That's not the gutweed," said Resus. "That smells like—"

A rasping noise made him look up. "Oh, no."

Luke squinted in the half light. Hundreds of tiny creatures were watching the trio with dull black eyes. "What," he asked, "are *they*?"

Resus pinched his nose as the vile smell got stronger. "Goblins!"

Chapter Ten
The Great Guff

The goblins crept toward them, leathery feet slapping against the bare stone of the floor. The nearer the creatures got, the fouler the smell became.

Luke pressed a hand over his nose and mouth. "What *is* that?"

"It's what makes goblins so delightful to be around," replied Cleo.

As if on cue, one of the goblins let rip a huge burst of gas from its bottom. The creature was propelled across the cavern, a cloud of green vapor trailing behind. It landed at Luke's feet and planted its hands firmly on its hips.

"I be Squiffer," it announced. "I be demand you no touch goblin 'longings!"

Resus grabbed the goblin and lifted it up to his face. "These *'longings*," he snarled, "have all been stolen by Sir Otto Sneer!"

Squiffer wriggled in Resus's hands. "Flabby man give 'longings to goblins."

"But they belong to the residents of Scream Street!"

"If pointy tooth cannot keep 'longings for himself," jeered Squiffer, "goblins will keep 'longings instead!"

Resus tightened his grip. "How about I show you just how pointy these teeth really are?" he hissed.

The goblin squealed and let out another blast of gas. "Don't be hurt Squiffer! Squiffer can be pointy tooth's friend!"

"That's better," said Resus as the stench subsided. "Now, we're not here for your 'longings.

We're looking for a relic. Something left behind by a vampire. Do you know where it is?"

Squiffer pulled a determined face. "Squiffer be not tell!"

"I thought you said you were going to be his friend," said Cleo.

The goblin stuck his tongue out at her. "Squiffer be change his mind. Squiffer be complicated that way!"

"Then who *will* tell us?" asked Resus. "Who's in charge here?"

"You be mean head of family?"

"Yes, I mean the head of the family!" snapped Resus. "Who is it?"

Squiffer nodded his head, moving it faster and faster until the nod became a violent shake. "I be no tell you that the Great Guff is head of family!" The goblin clamped a hand across its mouth, eyes wide as it realized it had given away the secret.

"I've had enough of this," said Luke. He snatched the creature from Resus and held it high. "I am a werewolf!" he shouted. "If the Great Guff does not reveal himself to me, I will transform and tear this goblin to pieces!"

Squiffer squealed
and pumped out
another noxious
green cloud,
forcing Luke to hold
his breath. A larger goblin
approached through
the mist, wearing
woollen baby
booties and a cape
made from tin foil.

"I be the Great
Guff," the goblin
announced. "Release Squiffer!"

Luke dropped the squirming creature. Before
it hit the ground, it let out another rip of gas that
propelled it across the cave. The terrified goblin
raced out into the sewer tunnel, screaming.

"You be want 'longing of way old pointy
tooth?" asked the Great Guff.

"Yes," Luke said, "we want 'longing of way
old pointy tooth. Where is it?"

"That be not the right question," said the
goblin. "Right question be, What you give the
Great Guff first?"

"You want me to give you something for telling me where the vampire's relic is?" Luke asked. The Great Guff smiled and held out his hand.

Luke clenched his fists. "But I don't have anything to give!"

The Great Guff turned away from Luke and folded his arms. "If wolf-boy be getting angry, the Great Guff be no tell!"

"I'm not angry," replied Luke, stuffing his hands into his pockets. "I just . . ." A smile spread across his face. "I just had to make sure you deserved my present. It can only be given to a great leader—if you know of one, that is."

The Great Guff gasped. "*I* be great leader! I be the Great Guff!"

"What a coincidence," said Luke, pulling the dog's collar from his pocket. The silver buckle glinted in the soft light. "Then this must be for you."

"What be that?" asked the Great Guff.

"This is a valuable necklace," said Luke. "Do you want it?"

The goblin watched the collar swing with greedy eyes. "Yes!" it breathed excitedly. "Give 'longing to the Great Guff!"

"OK," said Luke, "but there's one tiny adjustment to make." He turned to Resus. "I don't suppose you have a marker pen inside that cloak, do you?"

The vampire grinned. "A marker pen? Why, this is a virtual office supply store!" He reached inside his cape and hunted for the pen, handing Cleo a bicycle wheel and a toaster to hold while he dug deep into the pockets.

Eventually he produced a black felt-tip pen with a flourish. Luke took it and changed the name on the dog collar's tag from FLUFFY to GUFFY.

"Your Majesty," said Luke, bowing as he held out the collar. But the goblin's eyes were now fixed on something far more interesting: Resus's cloak.

"Why be the Great Guff want necklace when the Great Guff be having pointy tooth's cloak?" he said.

"I don't like the sound of this . . ." began Luke.

"Many 'longings in pointy tooth's cloak!"

"No! We agreed—"

"Goblins! Get 'longings!" screamed the Great

Guff. Bearing razor-sharp teeth, the pack of goblins attacked. Within seconds, Luke, Resus, and Cleo were overwhelmed by the tiny farting monsters.

Luke kicked one of the goblins in the stomach. It flew across the cavern, squealing as it crashed into a pile of board games and books. Another goblin instantly took its place, grabbing Luke's leg and biting hard.

Cleo was forced to the ground by the creatures as they rasped green fumes in her face. She pulled her bandages up to cover her mouth, but the dressing offered little protection and she felt her consciousness begin to slip away.

Resus pulled a golf club from his cloak and used it to drive the goblins away. "Fore!" he shouted as he whacked the creatures across the cave. But for every goblin he dispatched, three more leaped at him, and soon he, too, was covered in the stinking, biting creatures.

The green gas erupting from the goblins now enveloped Luke completely. Through streaming eyes he tried to locate his friends, but all he could see was even more goblins as they jumped on top of him.

"Resus!" he shouted. "Where are you?"

"Here!" yelled the vampire, biting into a goblin's bottom with his fangs and getting a cloud of green fumes in his face for his trouble.

"Cover your eyes!" called Luke in reply. "Cleo, you too!"

Cleo and Resus had no choice but to comply. They yanked their hands away from their goblin attackers and pressed them over their eyes as Luke lunged over to where he had heard Resus's voice.

Luke thrust his hand inside Resus's cape and pulled out the flaming torch. Closing his own eyes tightly, he plunged the torch deep into the center of the goblin gas cloud.

The cavern exploded.

When Luke opened his eyes, his first thought was of amazement that he could still operate any part of his body at all. The explosion had been far bigger than he had expected, and his ears were still ringing from the blast.

"Luke Watson," moaned Cleo as she came around and forced herself into a sitting position. "Since I met you, I've been burned, stabbed, and now blown up. . . . This is the most fun I've had in centuries!"

"My hair's all burned at the ends," complained Resus.

"Serves you right for dyeing it so much, doesn't it?" teased Cleo. "I knew that spray-on stuff wasn't good for you!"

"How do you know about that?"

"Resus, *everyone* knows," replied Cleo. "It's the worst-kept secret in Scream Street!" The vampire made a sulky face.

"Your hair *is* burned a bit, though," said Luke, reaching out to touch it. "Hey, is that a bald patch?"

The vampire slapped his hand away. "My fangs are still in full working order," he warned.

"Looks like the goblins came off worse," said Cleo. The tiny creatures were scattered across the floor of the cavern, an occasional *eep!* of green gas the only sign that they were still alive.

"We'd better get out of here before they wake up," said Resus.

"Look!" whispered Luke. In the center of the cave, clearly visible now that the goblins' stash of stolen items had been blown away, was a stone coffin.

"Do you think that's where the relic is?" asked Cleo, climbing to her feet.

Resus shrugged. "I guess we'll have to open it to be sure."

"I'll do it!" yelled Cleo, skipping across the cavern.

"And, somehow, it's always her that gets hurt. . . ." Resus grinned as he and Luke followed the mummy.

The trio gathered beside the coffin and pushed

at the stone lid. A scraping echoed around the cave as it shifted slightly.

"It's too heavy," said Luke. "We need something like a—"

"Crowbar?" asked Resus, pulling a long metal tool from his cloak.

Luke grinned. "It's no wonder the goblins are fans of your wardrobe!"

Using the crowbar, they were able to slide the heavy lid across the top of the coffin. Straining against the weight, Luke, Resus, and Cleo pushed with all their might until gravity took over and the slab of stone crashed to the floor.

The perfectly preserved body of a vampire lay inside, enshrouded in a black silk cloak. Resus gasped.

"It's Count Negatov!"

Chapter Eleven
The Fang

"I was only expecting the relic," said Luke. "Not the vampire himself."

"Is he dead?" asked Cleo, nudging Count Negatov's cheek with her finger.

"If he isn't, he'll have one heck of a stiff back when he gets up," said Resus. "According to the carvings on the coffin, he's been down here for over a century."

"Come on," said Luke, "let's find the relic and get out of here."

"I don't know. . . ." said Cleo. "It feels weird going through a dead vampire's pockets."

A cloud of gas appeared as one of the goblins rolled over and let rip.

"Maybe you'd prefer to wait until these guys wake up so you can ask them for help?" suggested Resus.

Cleo frowned. "Let's do it."

Luke lifted the edge of Count Negatov's cape and he, Cleo, and Resus slid their hands inside, exploring the cloak's many pockets.

"I've got something," said Luke. He pulled out a piece of parchment and unfurled it. "It looks like a family tree."

"Vampires are buried with details of their ancestors," explained Resus, "so that they can be easily identified in the next life."

"That doesn't help us find the relic," said Luke. "It's not here."

"Read the clue again," suggested Cleo.

Luke pulled *Skipstone's Tales of Scream Street* out of his pocket and opened it. The trio gathered around the book and read:

> In the tunnel, through the slime,
> the vampire lies for all of time;
> down where all is constant night,
> the source of power here will bite.

"It's his fangs," said Resus.

"Fangs?" asked Luke. "Are you sure?"

"The source of power here will bite," read Resus aloud. "The only part of a vampire that bites is his fangs."

"We have to take his teeth?" asked Cleo, disgusted.

Resus nodded. "It's the one thing that only a vampire can leave behind."

Luke stretched out his hand and carefully pushed back Count Negatov's top lip. The vampire's fangs glowed in the light of the gutweed. Luke took one of them between his fingers and pulled gently. It was stuck fast.

"Shame he's not wearing dentures, like you," Luke said. "There's no way they're coming out."

"Try this," suggested Resus, producing a pair of pliers from his cloak.

Cleo looked horrified. "You can't be serious!"

"Have you got any better ideas?" asked Resus. "We've got to do something before the farting army here wakes up."

Luke took the pliers and clamped hold of one of Count Negatov's fangs. "Do we need both of them?" he asked.

Resus shook his head. "A vampire needs his fangs to feed in the next life, so we'd better leave him one."

"Right," said Luke. "You two hold his head down and I'll pull."

Cleo and Resus positioned themselves at the top of the coffin and pressed their hands against the dead vampire's head. Cleo turned away, unable to watch.

"The good news," said Resus cheerfully, "is that he's been dead for over a century, so there shouldn't be any blood."

 102

Cleo kicked him in the shin. "You're enjoying this!" she snapped.

"OK," said Luke. "On three. One . . . two . . . three!"

In one swift movement, Cleo and Resus pushed down on the vampire's head as Luke gripped the pliers and pulled. With a sickening crack, the fang came free. A fountain of blood spurted from Count Negatov's mouth.

"You said there wouldn't be any blood!" Cleo squealed.

"There shouldn't be!" shouted Resus. "When vampires die, their blood evaporates. I don't understand it!"

As Luke held up the tooth to examine it, a hand shot out of the coffin and grabbed his throat. "I think I know why there's blood . . ." he gurgled.

"Who dares to disturb my rest?" demanded the vampire in a deep, solemn voice. His eyes were wide open, staring up at the children.

Luke swallowed hard. The vampire's grip on his throat was closing tighter. "My name is Luke Watson," he said in a strangled voice. "S-Samuel Skipstone sent me."

Count Negatov's eyes narrowed. "How do I know you speak the truth?"

Resus darted around the coffin until he was in the vampire's line of sight. "Count Negatov," he said. "I am Resus Negative, descendant of the glorious Negatov dynasty." He held his hand out toward the vampire.

Count Negatov studied the lines crossing Resus's palm. "You are indeed of the Negatov line," he said. "But who is he that has taken my fang?"

"He's a werewolf," explained Resus. "I'm helping him to collect the six relics of the founding fathers so that he can take his family out of Scream Street."

Count Negatov sighed. "For over a hundred years I have slept, awaiting the moment my relic would be collected. I have but one question. . . ." The vampire stared deep into Luke's eyes and asked, "Is he worthy of this gift?"

Resus smiled. "Yes, sire. He's my friend!"

The vampire released his grip on Luke's throat. "Then I may finally pass on to the next life," he said. "Your quest has received the blessing of the vampires."

Count Negatov closed his eyes for the final time and was silent.

Luke, Resus, and Cleo made their way back along the sewer tunnel, the flickering torch illuminating the fang as Luke studied it.

"Thank you," he said to Resus for the fifth time in as many minutes.

"It's no problem," said Resus. "You'd have done the same for me."

"Sorry to disturb such a touching moment,"

said Cleo, "but can we please get out of here so I can wash at least some of these stains out of my bandages?"

Luke grinned at her in the torchlight. "I think you look kinda cute," he said. "I hear mud brown and gutweed green are the in colors this season."

"If I wasn't so nice . . ." began Cleo. She stopped. "Shh! What's that?"

"What?" said Luke. "I can't hear anything."

"It's like wind," said Cleo. "Wind that's squeaking!"

Resus's cape flapped, and he struggled to keep hold of the torch as some unseen force threatened to pull it from his hands. "It's a poltergeist!" he shouted.

"Then what's squeaking?" asked Luke. The answer came as dozens of rats flew along the tunnel toward them, swept up by the poltergeist's power.

One of them gripped Luke's cheek as it bounced past, digging its claws into his skin to try to anchor itself. "Get it off me!" Luke yelled.

Resus reached inside his cloak and pulled out the first thing he could find: the crowbar. He swung it toward Luke's head, knocking the rat away but hitting his friend in the process.

"Ow!"

"Sorry!" Resus apologized.

"That really hurt!" said Luke, rubbing at his cheek. He pulled his hand away as blood began to run down his fingertips.

"That rat must have scratched you," said Cleo.

"No," said Luke. "It's not the rat." He gazed down at his fingernails as they stretched and grew, curling over to form powerful claws. "I'm changing!"

"Will it stop with your hands?" asked Resus. "I'm not crazy about being trapped underground with an angry werewolf!" The flaming torch was ripped from his hand. It clattered away down the tunnel, plunging the trio into blackness.

"Strike that," he shouted against the roar of the wind. "I'm not crazy about being trapped underground *in the dark* with an angry werewolf!"

The poltergeist attack was building. Rocks, twigs, and clumps of mud swirled around the confines of the tunnel.

"Hold on to me!" yelled Luke, digging his claws into the wall of the sewer pipe. Resus

gripped Luke's belt and offered Cleo the edge of
his cloak to hold. The ends of the mummy's bandages flapped out behind her.

Hand over hand, Luke dug his claws into the
brickwork of the tunnel, dragging himself and his
friends back toward the trapdoor. "I didn't think
the poltergeist's effects could be felt in the sewer!"

"Maybe someone knows we're down here,"
shouted Resus in reply.

"Impossible!" yelled Cleo. "Who could have
told Sir Otto where we are?"

Luke glanced over his shoulder. "Squiffer?"

"I've got a nice big cork in my cape," said the
vampire. "I'll stop up his behind for good, once
we get out of here!"

The trio finally reached the ladder that led
up to the cellar. As Luke climbed, the trapdoor
opened and he found himself staring into a familiar face. "Dr. Skully?"

"I thought you might need a hand with
Skipstone's quest," the skeleton said.

Dr. Skully reached down and helped Cleo to
clamber past the boys and out of the sewer. "But
you told us not to bother with Samuel Skipstone,"
she said.

"Changed my mind," said Dr. Skully, brushing aside his greasy red hair.

"You won't believe what we found down there, sir!" said Luke as he and Resus clambered out of the tunnel. "There's this massive cavern and—"

He froze. Dr. Skully didn't have red hair. . . .

Dixon's fist smashed into Luke's face, and the world went black.

Chapter Twelve
The Machine

Luke woke to find himself in a cage. He couldn't see much because the bars were covered in a sheet, and listening was proving pointless: all he could hear was the blood pumping through the worst headache he'd ever had.

He searched through his pockets, grunting in frustration. *Skipstone's Tales of Scream Street* and Count Negatov's fang had gone.

"There's a troll playing drums in my skull!" Resus lay beside him, clutching his head. "Where's my cloak?" he asked. "And where's Cleo?"

Luke was about to admit that he didn't know the answer to either question when the sheet was torn away. "You *know* where you are!" boomed a voice. "You've already been here — *to steal my book!*"

The cage had been set up in the secret room beneath Sir Otto's library. The landlord was holding *Skipstone's Tales of Scream Street* up to the bars. Dixon lurked behind him, wearing Resus's cape.

"However, as you've brought me a little gift, I'll accept your apology." Sir Otto produced Count Negatov's fang and clamped it under his lip. "Look at me, Dikthon!" he lisped. "I'm a vampire, just like our friend here!"

"Count Negatov will rise up and tear you apart!" roared Resus.

The landlord's face broke into a dark smile. "So, this *is* the fang of Negatov," he snarled. "Thank you for confirming my suspicions. Samuel

 111

Skipstone told me about the relics of the founding fathers. Soon their power will be mine!"

"That's not true!" shouted Luke. "Skipstone would never speak to you."

"That's what I thought too," said Sir Otto with a nasty grin, "but it would appear that I've been treating his book entirely the wrong way. I was trying to coax information out of Skipstone, when all I had to do was this. . . ."

Sir Otto opened the book and began to tear slowly at the corner of one of the pages. Samuel Skipstone screamed in agony. "I'm sorry, Luke," he cried. "He forced me to tell him about the relics!"

"I'll kill you," Luke yelled at Sir Otto. "I'll rip your heart out!"

"Which is exactly why I've got you locked in a cage," jeered the landlord.

"Where's Cleo?" demanded Resus.

"Ah, the mummy." Sir Otto sighed dramatically. "She proved to be quite the little fighter!" The landlord snapped his fingers.

Dixon pressed a series of buttons on a wall-mounted console. A section of the floor slid away to reveal a vast machine below. Cleo was strapped to the top of it.

"That's the generator!" cried Resus. "The generator that used to provide Scream Street with its electricity! I've seen pictures of it!"

"Only now its power has been adapted," said Sir Otto. "Instead of creating electricity, it drags the spirits of the dead from below and fuses them with energy!"

"You're — you're making poltergeists," said Resus. "You're not *controlling* the poltergeists; you're *making* them!"

"Clever, isn't it?" Sir Otto beamed proudly, stroking his silk scarf. "Who would have thought you freaks would be more use to me dead than alive?"

"The dead should be allowed to rest in peace!" shouted Resus.

"Which is why I've decided to experiment with a live specimen," said Sir Otto, gesturing toward Cleo. "By my calculations, the first blast of electricity should stop her heart, transferring control of her spirit directly to me."

"I'd like to see you try!" yelled Resus. "Her heart is—"

"My heart is in good condition," interrupted Cleo, throwing Resus a warning look. "Bring it

 113

on, Sneer," she teased. "Do your worst!"

The landlord thrust the fang and *Skipstone's Tales of Scream Street* into his pocket. "Oh, I do like it when they're feisty," he said with a grin. Then he waddled to the console and began adjusting a dial. The generator beneath Cleo started to hum.

"As soon as he flicks the switch, we move," whispered Luke to Resus. The vampire nodded, keeping his eyes fixed on Dixon as he checked the machine's cables.

Sir Otto turned. "Say good-bye to your organs, bandage girl!" He grinned, pulling the lever to turn the generator to full power.

Cleo's whole body jolted as the first blast of electricity roared through her. She barely had time to feel thankful that her heart and other organs were safe in her bedroom before another bolt of power brought with it a second shock.

"Now!" said Luke.

Using his fake fingernails, Resus picked the lock on the cage door. As Dixon realized what the vampire was doing, he rushed across the room to stop him, but he was too late.

114

The door hit Dixon full in the face, and he staggered to one side as Luke dashed out. Resus reached through the bars to grab his cloak. He pulled hard, and Dixon's skull hit the cage with a clang.

Dixon was stunned by the blow, forcing his shape-shifting mechanism into overdrive. Resus yanked back again and again, changing Sir Otto's nephew into Tibia Skully, Doug, and even Sir Otto himself as he bounced off the cage. Finally, just as the skinny man became Eefa Everwell, Resus tied his hair to the bars.

Sir Otto could hear nothing of the commotion behind him, the rattles and buzzes of the now fully active generator drowning out everything else. He continued to puff on his cigar and watch the dials of the machine.

As another surge of electricity passed through her body, Cleo looked up and saw Luke staring down at her from above. "I'm . . . fine . . ." she groaned through gritted teeth. "Get . . . the . . . fang!"

It wasn't until Luke was almost upon him that the landlord realized the cage was open. Turning,

Sir Otto punched Luke hard in the stomach. "You can't stop me," he shouted. "You and your pathetic parents are trapped here forever!"

Lashing out, Luke ripped the silk scarf away from the landlord's neck and froze. Sir Otto's throat was missing. Where there should have been skin was simply a tangled mass of flesh and bone, held together by strips of scar tissue.

"I grew up on this filthy street!" screamed Sir Otto. "My parents spent all their time making sure the monsters were happy. Even when I was attacked and *this* happened, the freaks always came first!" He held his cigar in front of Luke's face. "If it wasn't for the magic contained in these, I wouldn't be able to breathe at all!"

The landlord kicked Luke to the ground. "You freaks will pay," he spat. "When I have all the relics, I will banish everyone in this rotten street to the fires of the Underlands for all eternity!"

Luke felt the familiar sensation of change wash over him, but this was no partial trans-formation. His face stretched outward, teeth bursting from bloody gums. Claws ripped through the ends of his fingers as hair sprouted from his entire body.

Within seconds, Luke was in his full werewolf form. He leaped to his feet and advanced on Sir Otto, snarling.

The landlord grabbed a wrench from the toolbox at his feet and swung it at Luke, catching him on the shoulder. The wolf howled in pain and leaped forward, clamping its powerful jaws onto Sir Otto's arm and biting hard.

The wrench struck Luke across the face this time, sending him crashing to the floor. The landlord snatched up the entire toolbox and hurled it. The werewolf twisted to one side, and the heavy metal box smashed harmlessly beside him.

A scream rang out. "Resus!" cried Cleo. "Something's happening!"

Resus banged Dixon's head against the cage one final time and turned to peer down at Cleo. Smoke was beginning to rise from the mummy's bandages.

"There's something else here," shouted Cleo. "No—some*one*! The machine's pulling another spirit up from the dead!"

Resus raced for the control panel as the generator started to shake violently.

The battle between Luke and Sir Otto

continued to rage. The wolf's jaws snapped together again and again as the landlord lashed out with the wrench. Sir Otto lunged at Luke. The wolf leaped into the air, and the landlord crashed into a bank of machinery, becoming entangled in the wiring.

Luke leaped on top of Sir Otto and howled, baring his teeth for the kill. The landlord screamed and closed his eyes as the wolf lunged forward. There was a rip as Luke tore open Sir Otto's pocket, grabbing both *Skipstone's Tales of Scream Street* and Count Negatov's fang with his teeth.

Luke climbed off the landlord and growled.

 118

Sir Otto sobbed helplessly. The wolf, content the fight was over, padded over to where Cleo was strapped down.

"Stop the generator, Resus!" bellowed Cleo. "It's coming!"

"I'm trying!" shouted Resus, flicking switch after switch. The vampire could only watch as light began to shine from the gaps between Cleo's bandages.

A roar filled the room. Sir Otto, who had only been pretending to cry, charged at Luke. The wolf flipped onto his back and thrust his legs in the air, pressing them hard into the landlord's stomach.

Kicking with all his might, Luke flipped Sir Otto over his head and down toward the generator below. The landlord crashed on top of the machine, smashing Cleo's restraints and allowing her to wriggle to one side just as a fully formed poltergeist burst out of the generator with a scream.

Resus watched in horror as the bolt of pure energy shot through the air toward Luke. He dived toward his friend and snatched *Skipstone's Tales of Scream Street* from the wolf's jaws. He used the metallic silver cover to deflect the screeching ghost across the room and into the control panel on the wall.

The console exploded. Cables and wires fizzed with energy as the poltergeist was fed back into the machine that had created it.

The generator dropped to a low hum, Cleo slumped back against the unconscious landlord, and Resus watched in amazement as the single electric lightbulb that hung from the ceiling flickered into life.

Chapter Thirteen
The Gift

"This way," said Resus to the line that snaked through his house and down into the cellar. Luke was in the sewer tunnel below, passing up books, paintings, and ornaments as the residents of Scream Street came to reclaim what Sir Otto had confiscated from them.

"Any sign of the goblins?" the vampire called down through the trapdoor.

Luke shook his head. "I guess they don't feel safe down here anymore."

"Not since you tried to blow them up, anyway." Resus grinned. He glanced over his shoulder as Eefa Everwell arrived. "How's Cleo?"

"She'll be fine," said the witch. "She's in bad shape at the moment, but after a few days' bed rest, she'll be running around like normal."

"I hope not," said Resus. "We're getting a bit fed up with having to rescue her every ten minutes, aren't we?" He glanced at Luke to find his friend staring at Eefa, once again lost in her enchantment. Resus laughed. "You'd better close your mouth in case another rat comes flying by!"

Dr. Skully and Alston Negative appeared beside Luke in the tunnel. "That's the last of the items," said the teacher. "Now, if you and Resus would be good enough to show us where this secret room is . . ."

Dixon opened the gates to Sneer Hall without complaint. "I'm sorry," he whined, rubbing at the bald patches on his head. "Uncle Otto made me do it!"

"Where is he now?" asked Luke.

"In his room," replied Dixon. "He says he won't come out for anyone."

"That'll save us some trouble," said Alston.

Luke led the way to Sir Otto's library and pulled the book out from its position on the shelf. With a click, the secret door opened.

"A basic pulley mechanism," said Dr. Skully, examining the bookcase. "Shouldn't be too difficult to disable. This door won't be used again."

Alston followed Luke and Resus down the steps and into the stone room. Clumps of red hair were still knotted around the bars of the cage.

"Looks like Dixon had to pull himself free to get to Sir Otto," said Resus.

"He must have been tearing his hair out with worry!" Luke quipped.

Alston checked the settings on the control panel, pressing various buttons to ensure the dials were reading as they should. "It all looks to be in working order," he said. "Blasting that poltergeist back into the machine must have tripped the reset switch and set it running in the right direction again."

"So, Scream Street's going to get its electricity supply back?" asked Resus.

"As long as the wiring is still intact," replied Alston. "I've got someone checking that as we speak."

A handful of stone crumbled from the wall, and a green head appeared, a screwdriver clenched between rotten teeth. "Everything looks hunky-dory to me, dudes!" Doug grinned. "Fire her up!"

Alston pulled a lever on the console, and the generator rattled to life.

"Uh-oh!" said Doug, sniffing the air. "I think something's burning. . . ."

Luke held his nose. "That's not burning," he said. Snatching up the sheet that had covered the cage, he found Squiffer crouched there, hiding behind his hands. Luke grabbed him, causing the terrified goblin to let off another blast of noxious gas.

"You be leave me alone!" Squiffer screeched. "Or I be go and tell flabby man about you!"

"I think you've told Sir Otto enough," said Luke. "Although I agree that you should probably spend a bit more quality time together!"

Resus and Luke climbed the stairs and followed the stench of cigars to Sir Otto's bedroom. He opened the door to discover the landlord lying on his bed, an ice pack on his head and a face mask over his eyes.

"Is that you, Dixon?" Sir Otto growled without looking up. "I thought I told you that I didn't want to be disturbed!"

Squiffer let loose a silent burst of gas, and Luke was forced to cover his mouth, both against the stench and for fear of laughing.

"Well, seeing as you're here now," continued the landlord, "see if you can do something about the drains. Since those impudent young freaks invaded the sewers, the pipes have stunk like a troll's armpit!"

"I've always said it takes one bad smell to know another," said Luke.

Sir Otto ripped the mask from his eyes. "You!"

"We came to see how you're feeling," said Resus. "It can't be nice having a poltergeist pass right through you."

"Maybe that's where they get their famous tempers from?" Luke grinned.

"I'll get you!" roared the landlord, struggling to climb off the bed.

Luke made a face. "And to think, we came to bring an old friend for a visit!" He tossed Squiffer into the room and slammed the door. Resus slid a fake fingernail into the lock and closed it with a click.

"No!" screamed Sir Otto, rattling the door as an *eep!* escaped from the goblin. "Get me away from this thing. Let me out!"

Resus smiled as wafts of green cloud seeped beneath the door. "Do you think they'll be OK in there?"

Luke nodded. "Trust me," he said. "They'll have a gas!"

Luke sat on the edge of his bed, blasting the evil army of mechanoids that invaded his gamepad. Since the electricity supply had been restored, the residents of Scream Street had been pulling all kinds of appliances out of retirement. Luke was just happy his games were working again.

He reached the end of the level and pressed

a series of buttons to activate his rocket launcher as the robot overlord hovered into view.

"These moving stories really are very exciting!" exclaimed Samuel Skipstone from the cover of his book on the bedside table. "And I used to think pencil illustrations were advanced!"

There was a knock at the door. "Come in," called Luke, pausing the game.

Mr. and Mrs. Watson entered the room with a tray of food. Luke didn't need his werewolf sense of smell to identify the dinner: cheeseburger and fries.

"How are you feeling?" Luke asked his mom, indicating her bandaged arm.

"I'll live," she said.

Luke's dad jumped as a skeletal dog burst into the room and leaped up at him, barking. Cleo and Resus appeared in the doorway. "Scapula wanted to come and say hello," explained the mummy. She was wrapped in fresh white bandages and had applied makeup to those across her face.

Resus had redyed his hair jet black and smoothed it all down with gel. His face was once again coated in white face paint, and his cloak had a new electric-blue lining.

 127

"We'll leave you to it," said Mr. Watson, throwing Resus a nervous glance.

"Your dad's still not sure about me," said the vampire with a grin as the door closed.

"I guess it's the whole 'creature of the night' image," said Luke. "You do look pretty scary!"

Resus grinned. "I just have to work out how to hide my reflection in mirrors now. That'll *really* spook people!"

Cleo nudged the vampire. "Go on," she said. "Give it to him."

"You give it to him!" said Resus.

"Will one of you tell me what's going on?" said Luke.

Resus shrugged and pulled open his cape. Cleo reached inside and produced a small golden casket. "We thought this would be ideal to keep the book and the relic in until we find the others." She smiled.

Luke took the casket and ran his hands over the hieroglyphics carved into the lid. "Wait a minute," he said. "Isn't this where you keep—?"

"My heart, liver, and kidneys—yes!" Cleo beamed. "But they're better off in the fridge now that the power's back on."

 128

Luke pulled Count Negatov's fang from the pocket of his jeans and dropped it into the casket. "I don't know what to say."

"Scapula!" shouted Resus.

"No, it definitely isn't that," said Luke.

"Scapula, put that down!" yelled Resus. Luke turned to see the dog heading for the door, *Skipstone's Tales of Scream Street* in his mouth.

"Oh, dear!" cried Samuel Skipstone. "I do not like this at all!"

"Scapula!" called Luke, Resus, and Cleo as they chased the dog down the stairs, through the front door, and out into Scream Street.

Luke's quest continues in:

SCREAM STREET

Book Two
BLOOD OF THE WITCH

Turn the page to read
the first chapter. . . .

Chapter One
The Blood

Blood trickled down the vampire's fangs. A long tongue flicked out and licked the sticky fluid from sharp, glistening teeth. The vampire's mouth twisted into a smile as it savored the taste. It wanted more.

Lashing out, the vampire used its yellowing talons to tear another hunk of meat from the carcass. Pausing only to drench it in the nearby pool of blood, the creature bit into strips of flesh, veins

An excerpt from *Book Two: Blood of the Witch*

and tendons swinging below its salivating jaw. Suddenly a cry rang out.

"Dad! Leave some for everyone else!"

Alston Negative glanced around the dinner table and slowly placed the chicken wing back onto his plate. "Sorry," he mumbled, shamefaced.

Resus Negative, the vampire's son, reached inside his electric-blue-lined cape and produced a knife and fork. Handing them to his father, he added, "And you know you should be using silverware when we have visitors."

As Alston fumbled with the unfamiliar tools, Resus nudged his friend Luke Watson. "You don't make that much mess when you eat—and you're a werewolf!"

Luke grinned as he watched the older vampire push the chicken wing off his plate, catapulting potatoes across the black dining-room carpet.

"Being a vampire does have its advantages," joked Alston, leaping from his chair. "When I'm tired of biting necks, I double as a vegetable rack!" He pecked at the carpet and reappeared with a potato stuck to each fang.

"Dad," groaned Resus, embarrassed. "You're not funny!"

🦇 An excerpt from *Book Two: Blood of the Witch*

Luke roared with laughter and turned to his parents to share the joke. His face fell when he realized that the get-together hadn't worked. His mom and dad were still terrified of their vampire neighbors.

An excerpt from *Book Two: Blood of the Witch* 🦇

"A toast!" exclaimed Alston, pulling the potatoes from his teeth and raising a glass of wine. "To the Watsons, and your first week in Scream Street!"

"The Watsons!" echoed Resus, lifting his tumbler of milk. He clinked it against Luke's and drank deeply, his fangs tinkling against the rim of the glass. Instead of drinking his own milk, Luke reached out to take his mom's trembling hand and guide it toward her wine.

Mrs. Watson forced a smile. "Thank you," she whispered hoarsely.

Luke and Resus shared a glance. Luke's family had been moved to Scream Street by G.H.O.U.L., Government Housing of Unusual Life-forms, after he had transformed into his werewolf form and attacked a school bully. Since then, his parents had lived in a state of sheer terror.

In order to open a doorway back to his own world, Luke had begun to search for six relics left behind by the community's founding fathers. The first of these, a vampire's fang, was now locked away in a golden casket under his bed.

"Now," said Bella Negative as she entered, carrying a jug of thick red liquid, "who wants more blood on their meat?"

An excerpt from *Book Two: Blood of the Witch*

Mr. Watson stared at the jug and paled. "I think I'm going to be sick. . . ."

"I'll get you some water," said Luke, racing to the kitchen. Reaching for the cold tap, he stopped. The sink had three taps. "Resus!" he called.

The young vampire hurried in. "You summoned me?" he teased.

"Which one is cold water?" Luke asked.

"Isn't it obvious?" replied Resus. He gestured from left to right. "Hot water, cold water, blood."

"Blood?" exclaimed Luke. "You've got a tap for *blood*?"

"Of course," said Resus. "How else do you think vampires get their fix? We need a regular supply." He spun the tap, allowing a torrent of crimson blood to flow out into the sink. It spattered against the stainless steel, leaving behind small clots and scabs as it raced for the drain.

"B-but a *tap*?" stammered Luke. "Where does it come from?"

"Whenever anyone has a nosebleed or a cut finger and they rinse away the blood, it ends up in the sewer system," explained Resus. "The blood is filtered out and fed to vampires around the world."

An excerpt from *Book Two: Blood of the Witch*

"That's disgusting!"

"No more disgusting than the way our ancestors used to get it." Resus opened his mouth and bared his fangs at Luke with a hiss.

Bella Negative appeared behind him. "Getting a drink of blood?" she asked, ruffling her son's hair.

"Luke knows I'm a normal like his mom and dad," Resus sighed. "He knows I'm not a real vampire!" He unclipped his false fangs and rinsed them briefly under the water before reattaching them to his teeth. Suddenly the stream of blood stopped, the last remaining drips pattering against the sink.

"That's odd," said Resus. He opened the cupboard under the sink and reached past boxes of coffin polish and fang whitener to check the pipes.

Luke crouched down beside him. "Maybe there's a safety campaign going on and people have stopped skinning their knees." He grinned.

"I hope not," said Resus. "My dad gets really cranky without his daily pint!"

"Er, Luke," called Alston from the dining room, "I think your parents are ready to go home now."

🦇 An excerpt from *Book Two: Blood of the Witch*

Luke stood and turned to see his mom smiling bravely, his dad's arm tight around her shoulders. "I've got to take them away from here," he said quietly to Resus. "They're never going to be happy as long as we're in Scream Street."

"You mean . . . ?" began the young vampire.

Luke nodded. "It's time to find the second relic."

An excerpt from *Book Two: Blood of the Witch*